GLASSES FOR D.W.

朵拉也想戴眼镜

（美）马克·布朗　绘著

范晓星　译

CHISO 新疆青少年出版社

Arthur wore glasses.

"I wish I wore glasses too,"
said his little sister, D.W.
"They look cool."

"But I really need them
to see," said Arthur.
"Before I wore glasses,
things looked funny."

"A hat looked like…

a bat.

Some string looked like…

a ring.

Some trash looked like…

some cash.

A log looked like…

a dog," said Arthur.

"Things look funny
to me too," said D.W.

"Remember last summer
when I saw the shark
at the beach…"

"...and no one else did?
The nice lifeguard said,
'Maybe you need glasses,
little girl,'" said D.W.

"And Mom always tells me
I can't see what a mess
my room is," said D.W.
"Maybe glasses would help."

"You need more than glasses
to clean up that mess,"
said Arthur.

"I never can find my toothbrush,"
said D.W.
"And Daddy says
it's because I'm blind as a bat.
See, that means I need glasses."

"No," said Arthur.

"It just means you don't like

to brush your teeth."

"I REALLY do need glasses!"

said D.W.

She took two steps

and bumped into the lamp.

She took three more steps
and bumped into Arthur.
"I can't even see YOU, Arthur!"
cried D.W.

"Try opening your eyes,"
said Arthur.

Just then Arthur's friend Buster

came over.

"D.W. is acting silly,"

Arthur said to Buster.

D.W. took two steps

and bumped into Buster.

"Buster? Is that you?"

she said.

"Guess what? I can't see!"

"So I'm getting glasses!"

said D.W.

"Orange glasses that sparkle…

love glasses…

sunglasses…

rainglasses…

zillions of glasses!"

Buster gave D.W. a funny look.

"She's nuts, Arthur,"

said Buster. "Come on,

let's play soccer."

D.W. opened her eyes.

"I want to play too,"

she said.

"You can't play soccer

if you can't see,"

said Arthur.

D.W. grabbed the soccer ball.

She bounced it up and down.

"Who says I can't see?"

said D.W.

"Hooray!" yelled Arthur.

"She can see again.

It's the miracle soccer cure!"

"But I still want glasses,"
said D.W.

2. 亚瑟戴上了一副眼镜。

"我也好想戴眼镜哦，"妹妹朵拉说，"你的眼镜看起来特别酷。"

3. "可我是真的需要戴眼镜啊，"亚瑟回答，"我不戴眼镜的时候，看什么都怪怪的。"

4. "帽子看上去像是……一只蝙蝠。

绳子看上去像是……一枚戒指。

5. 垃圾看上去像是……一堆零钱。

木头看上去像是……一只小狗。"亚瑟说。

6. "我看东西也是怪怪的。"朵拉说。

7. "你还记得吧，去年夏天只有我在海边看见一头鲨鱼……

8. "……其他人都没看见。当时那个好脾气的救生员还对我说：'小姑娘，看来你需要戴一副眼镜了哦。'"朵拉说。

10. "妈妈不是也总说我看不见我的房间有多乱吗？"朵拉又说，"我要是戴上一副眼镜就能看见了。"

11. "你最需要的不是戴眼镜，而是打扫房间！"亚瑟回应。

12. "我总也找不到牙刷，"朵拉又说，"爸爸说那是因为我就像蝙蝠一样什么都看不见。瞧，这不是也说明我需要戴眼镜吗？"

13. "才不是呢！"亚瑟回答，"那只能说明你不喜欢刷牙！"

14. "我真的需要戴眼镜！"朵拉说着，走上前两步，碰翻了落地灯。

15. 接着，朵拉又走上前三步，撞到了亚瑟身上。

"我看不见你了，亚瑟！"朵拉大声喊。

"睁开眼睛吧。"亚瑟回应。

16. 这时，亚瑟的好朋友巴斯特走了进来。

"朵拉在出洋相哦。"亚瑟对巴斯特说。

17. 朵拉又走上前两步，撞到了巴斯特身上。

"巴斯特，是你吗？"她说，"你知道吗？我什么都看不见啦！"

28

18. "这样我就可以戴眼镜了！"朵拉说。

"橘红色的、亮晶晶的小眼镜……爱心小眼镜……

19. 太阳镜……

挡雨镜……
还有各种各样的小眼镜！"

20. 巴斯特朝朵拉做了一个鬼脸，对亚瑟说：

"她疯了，亚瑟！走，咱们踢足球去。"

21. 朵拉睁开眼睛说："我也想玩儿。"

22. "你看不见，不能踢球。"亚瑟回应。

朵拉抢过足球，"啪啪"地拍起来。

23. "谁说我看不见了？"朵拉说。

"万岁！"亚瑟高兴地喊，"朵拉又能看见了，真是神奇的足球疗法呀！"

24. "可我还是想要戴眼镜。" 朵拉回应。